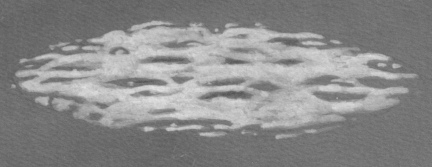

CUENTO
DE LUZ

To my traveling companions.
— Roberto Aliaga —

To Mary and her grandparents, who illuminate my way.
— Miguel Ángel Díez —

This book is printed on **Stone Paper** with silver **Cradle to Cradle**™certification.
Cradle to Cradle™ is one of the most demanding ecological certification systems, awarded to products that have been conceived and designed in an ecologically intelligent way.

Cradle to Cradle™ recognizes that environmentally safe materials are used in the manufacturing of Stone Paper which have been designed for re-use after recycling. The use of less energy in a more efficient way, together with the fact that no water, trees nor bleach are required, were decisive factors in awarding this valuable certification.

Fireflies
Text © 2019 Roberto Aliaga
Illustrations © 2019 Miguel Ángel Díez
This edition © 2019 Cuento de Luz SL
Calle Claveles, 10 | Urb. Monteclaro | Pozuelo de Alarcón | 28223 | Madrid | Spain
www.cuentodeluz.com
Title in Spanish: *Luciernágas*
English translation by Jon Brokenbrow
Printed in PRC by Shanghai Chenxi Printing Co., Ltd. March 2019, print number 1673-4
ISBN: 978-84-16733-54-5

Fireflies

Roberto Aliaga   Miguel Ángel Díez

In the blink of an eye, Firefly Field wasn't
a field anymore, and it didn't belong to
the fireflies. Without a home, without
food, and without a future, the fireflies
made a decision. They packed their bags,
and for the first time ever in the history
of their species, leaving behind their
homes and their memories, they set off in
search of the light at the end of the way.

They all left together.

At the start of the journey, the littlest fireflies played tag. The young fireflies talked together and made plans. The adults argued over the maps and where they were heading. And the oldest fireflies … kept silent.

Darkness fell, and it became terribly cold.
Luke suddenly realized he'd forgotten
something. It was so important, he began
to cry. He rummaged through his suitcase,
but it wasn't there.

"We can't go on!" he said.

He called to his family, "Daddy, we have
to go back! I've forgotten my teddy!"

The members of his family looked at each other, and smiled.

"Don't worry. Everything will turn out all right," said his sister Lucy, gently.

She pointed into the distance.

"Look at that light, all the way over there. Once we reach it, there'll be other teddies for you!"

But when they arrived at the light, it didn't seem to be the destination they'd all dreamed of.

"Where are the teddies, Lucy?" asked Luke.

Some of the fireflies stayed there, but the rest of them picked up their bags again and slowly continued with their journey, in search of the light at the end of the way.

Darkness fell, and with it a feeling of loneliness. Lucy suddenly realized she'd lost something. It was so important, she began to cry. She flew all the way through the column of fireflies, but she couldn't find them.

"We can't go on!" she said.

She called to her family, "Daddy, we have to go back! I can't find Claire, or Aurora, or … "

The members of her family looked at each other, and smiled.

"Don't worry. Everything will turn out all right," said her father, gently.

He pointed into the distance. "Look at that light. Once we reach it, you'll find new friends."

But when they arrived at the light, it didn't seem to be the destination they'd all dreamed of.

"Where are my friends?" asked Lucy.

Some of the fireflies stayed there, but the rest of them picked up their bags and slowly continued with their journey, in search of the light at the end of the way.

Darkness fell, and with it a feeling of fear. Their father suddenly realized there was a problem. It was so important, he began to cry. He looked at his compass, his maps, and the position of the stars.

"We can't go on!" he said.

He called to the rest of the family. "We're lost!"

The members of the family exchanged glances, and some of them had tears in their eyes.

"Don't worry, my boy. Everything will turn out all right," said Grandma sweetly.

She pointed into the distance. "Look at those lights. Once we reach them, we'll know where we are, and we can continue on our way."

But when they arrived at the lights, it didn't seem to be the destination they'd all dreamed of.

"I don't know where we'll go now," said their father.

But they picked up their bags anyway, and continued into the darkness, searching for the light at the end of the way.

Darkness fell, and with it a feeling of exhaustion. Grandma realized she couldn't go on any further. It was so important, she didn't shed a tear. She stopped next to a stone, and sighed.

"You go on," she said. "Carry on without me. I've reached the end of the way. My light is going out."

The members of the family looked at each other sadly, and they began to cry. All of them, except Luke.

"Don't worry, Grandma. Everything will be all right!" he said sweetly.

He pointed at himself. "Look at me! I'm here! We're nearly there . . . and you and me together have all the light in the world!"

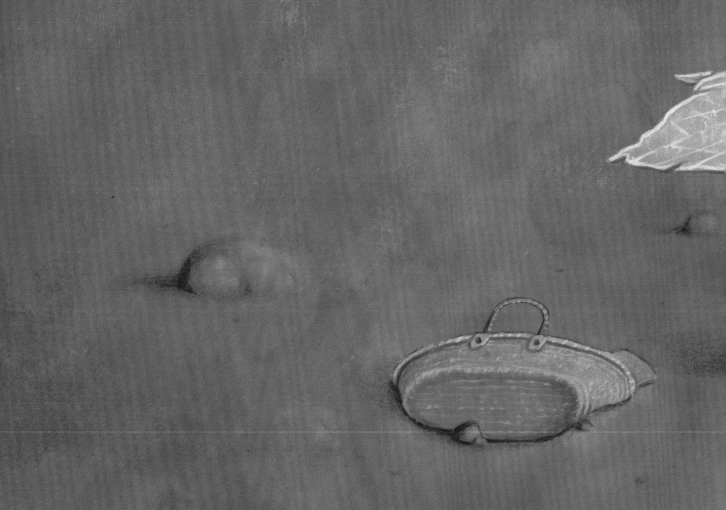

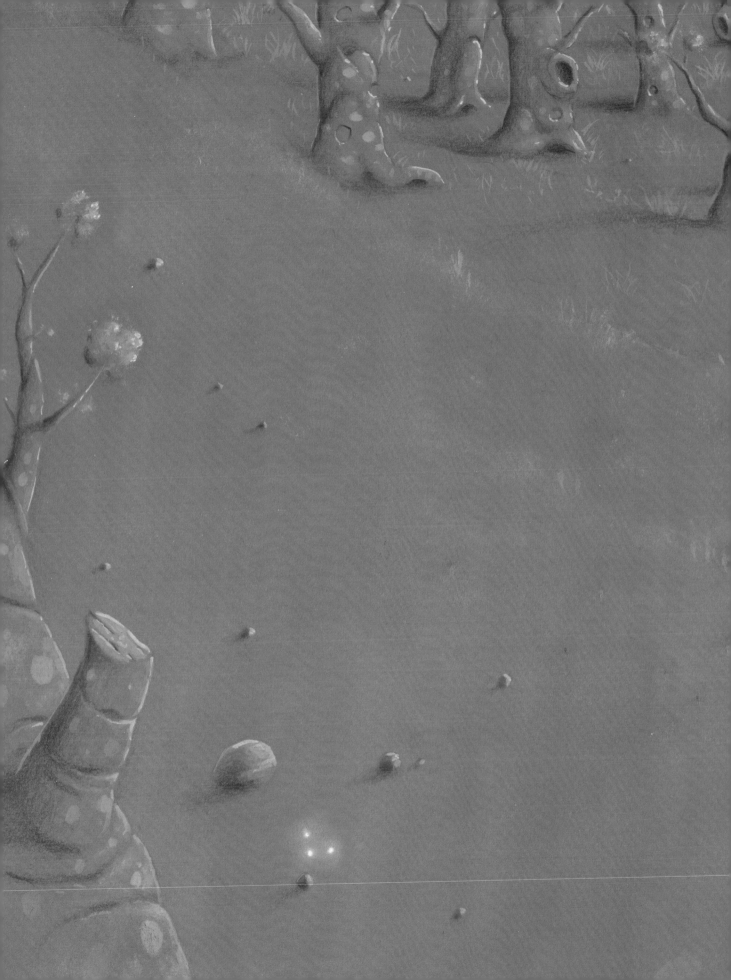

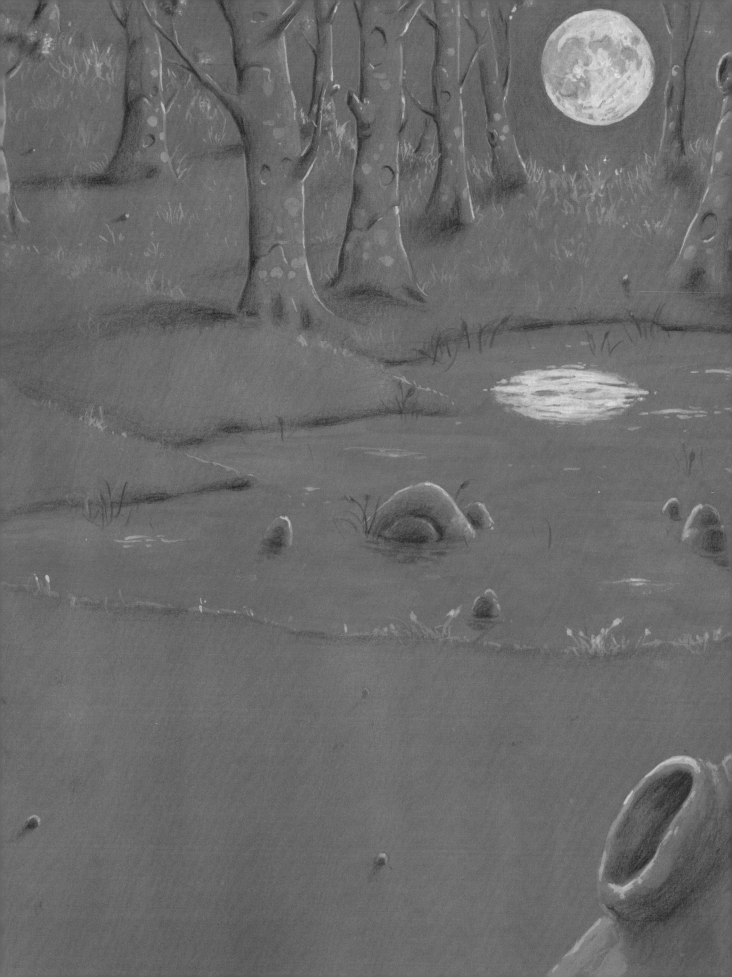